# Oi PUPPIES!

Written by
**Kes Gray**

Illustrated by
**Jim Field**

*Hodder
Children's
Books*

**BARK!**

**YAP!**

**YAP, YAP!**

**BARK!**

"I'm looking after some puppies," said the dog.

"How many puppies?" frowned the frog.

"Quite a lot of puppies," gulped the dog.

This one's called
**Tiddle.**

This one's called
**Buster.**

That one's
called **Rover.**

"This one's
called
**Jock.**

And this
one's called
**Milo.**"

"SIT, MILO!" said the cat.

"He won't sit," said the dog.

"SIT, TIDDLE!" said the frog.

"She won't sit either," said the dog.

"Why won't they **SIT?**" asked the cat.

"Because they're puppies," said the dog.
"Puppies are far too busy being puppies to sit."

"Not these puppies," said the dog.

"These puppies are really badly trained."

"There's a puppy hanging from my whiskers," frowned the cat.

"He's called **Spot,**" said the dog.

"There's a puppy chewing my swimming trunks," said the frog.

"She's called **Lollie,**" said the dog.

"What are *these* puppies called?"
asked the frog.

**"Tickle, Blue, Scamp, Rebel, Smudge**
and **Shep,"** said the dog.

"And what are *these* puppies called?" frowned the cat.

**"Winnie, Cheeky, Spike, Flash, Trubble,
and Trixie,"** said the dog.

# "WELL, DO SOMETHING ABOUT THEM!"

yelled the cat.

"Let me make a phone call,"
said the frog.

"Where do you want everything?"
said the delivery duck.

"On the next page,
please," said the frog.

"Buster's on a **duster,**

Jock's on a **clock,**

and **Tiddle** is on a **fiddle!**"

Milo's on a **lilo,**

"That's not all," smiled the cat.

Tickle's on some **pickles,**

and Smudge is on some **fudge!"**

"Rover's on some **clover,**

PICKLES

"I wonder what **Spot** is sitting on?" said the dog.

"**Spot** is on a **yacht**," said the frog.

"**Spot's** on a **yacht**,

**Shep's** on a **step**,

*The Waggy Tail*

**Rebel's** on a **pebble**,

Scamp's on a **lamp,**

**Cheeky** is on some **tzatziki,**

and **Blue's** on a **shoe."**

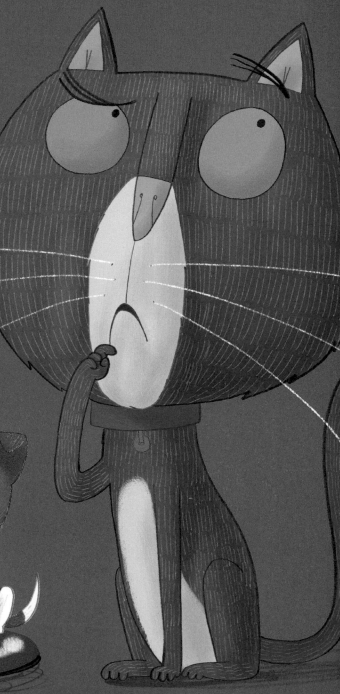

"I wonder what **Lollie** is sitting on?" said the cat.

"**Lollie's** on a **trolley**," said the frog.

"Lollie's on a
**trolley**,

Trixie's
on a
**pixie**,

Flash
is on a
**splash,**

**Spike's**
on a
**trike,**

Winnie's
on a
**pinny,**

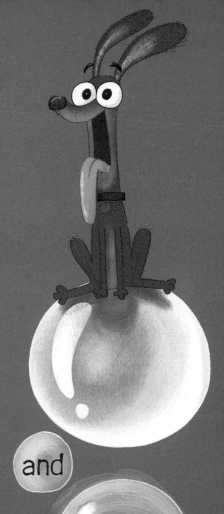

and

**Trubble**

is

on

a

**bubble."**

"That's amazing!"
said the dog.

"Hold on, what do **tadpoles** sit on?" said the dog.

"And **kittens** that are **allergic** to **mittens?**" said the cat.

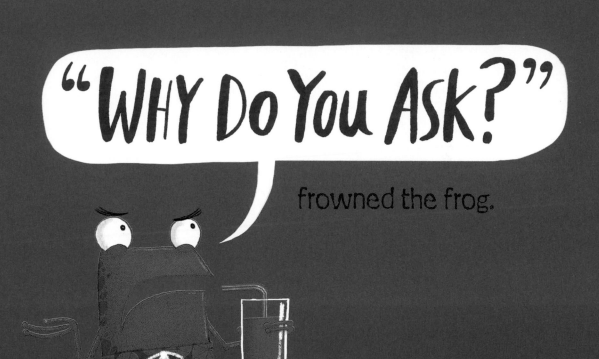

"**WHY Do You Ask?**"

frowned the frog.

“Oi TAXI!”
yelled the frog.
MY NAME IS ORANGE!”
“MY NAME IS LEMON!”
M MIFFYMOPS!”
“I’M CUTEYKINS!”
“MY NAME IS DIDDLY!”
“MY NAME IS SQUIGGLY!”

**To Dexter, Amanda and Lottie  K.G.**
**For the libraries and the librarians. Thank you!  J.F.**

HODDER CHILDREN'S BOOKS
First published in Great Britain in 2019 by Hodder and Stoughton
This paperback edition first published in 2020

Text copyright © Kes Gray, 2019
Illustrations copyright © Jim Field, 2019

The moral rights of the author and illustrator have been asserted.
All rights reserved

PB ISBN: 978 1 444 93736 7

3 5 7 9 10 8 6 4

Printed and bound in China

Hodder Children's Books
An imprint of Hachette Children's Group
Part of Hodder and Stoughton
Carmelite House, 50 Victoria Embankment
London, EC4Y 0DZ

An Hachette UK Company
www.hachette.co.uk
www.hachettechildrens.co.uk

www.kesgray.com
www.jimfield.co.uk